A Note to Parents and Caregivers:

Read-it! Joke Books are for children who are moving ahead on the amazing road to reading. These fun books support the acquisition and extension of reading skills as well as a love of books.

Published by the same company that produces *Read-it!* Readers, these books introduce the question/answer pattern that helps children expand their thinking about language structure and book formats.

When sharing a book with your child, read in short stretches, pausing often to talk about the pictures and the meaning of the book. The question/answer format works well for this purpose and provides an opportunity to talk about the language and meaning of the jokes. Have your child turn the pages and point to the pictures and familiar words. Read the story in a natural voice; have fun creating the voices of characters or emphasizing some important words. And be sure to reread favorite parts.

There is no right or wrong way to share books with children. Find time to read with your child, and pass on the legacy of literacy.

Adria F. Klein, Ph.D.
Professor Emeritus
California State University
San Bernardino, California

Managing Editor: Bob Temple
Creative Director: Terri Foley
Editors: Brenda Haugen, Nadia Higgins
Designer: John Moldstad
Page production: Picture Window Books
The illustrations in this book were prepared digitally.

Picture Window Books
5115 Excelsior Boulevard
Suite 232
Minneapolis, MN 55416
1-877-845-8392
www.picturewindowbooks.com

Printed in the United States of America.

Library of Congress Cataloging-in-Publication Data
Dahl, Michael.
Who's there? : a book of knock-knock jokes / written by Michael Dahl ;
illustrated by Ryan Haugen ; reading advisers, Adria F. Klein, Susan Kesselring.
p. cm. – (Read-it! joke books)
ISBN 1-4048-0233-9
1. Knock-knock jokes. I. Haugen, Ryan, 1972- II. Title.
PN6231.K55 D439 2003
818'.602-dc21
                                                          2003004872

Who's There?

A Book of Knock-Knock Jokes

Michael Dahl • Illustrated by Ryan Haugen

Reading Advisers:
Adria F. Klein, Ph.D.
Professor Emeritus, California State University
San Bernardino, California

Susan Kesselring, M.A., Literacy Educator
Rosemount-Apple Valley-Eagan (Minnesota) School District

PICTURE WINDOW BOOKS
Minneapolis, Minnesota

Knock knock.
    Who's there?
Dwayne.
    Dwayne who?

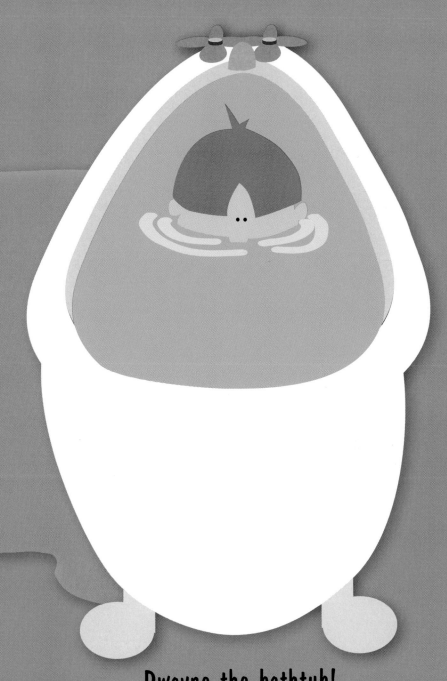

Dwayne the bathtub!
I'm dwowning!

5

Knock knock.
    Who's there?
Amos.
    Amos who?

A mosquito bit me.

Knock knock.
    Who's there?
Annie.
    Annie who?

Annie bit me again!   7

Knock knock.
   Who's there?
Yah.
   Yah who?

8   I didn't know you were a cowboy.

Knock knock.
Who's there?
Dishes.
Dishes who?

Dishes your friend. So open the door. 9

Knock knock.
    Who's there?
Cows go.
    Cows go who?

No, cows go, "Moo."

Knock knock.
Who's there?
Hutch.
Hutch who?

Cover your mouth
when you sneeze!

Knock knock.
 Who's there?
Anita.
 Anita who?

Anita tissue.

Knock knock.
  Who's there?
Butter.
  Butter who?

Butter bring an umbrella.
It looks like rain.

14

Knock knock.
  Who's there?
Wayne.
  Wayne who?

Wayne, Wayne, go away.
Come again another day.   15

Knock knock.
Who's there?
Sarah.
Sarah who?

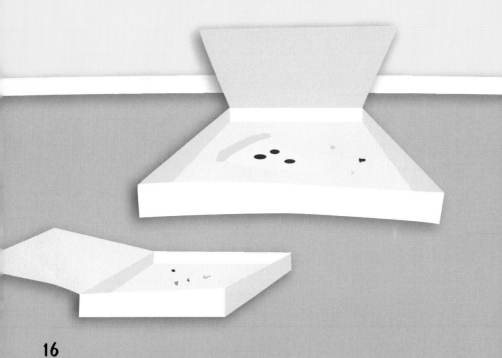

Sarah piece of pizza left? 17

Knock knock.
   Who's there?
Oswald.
   Oswald who?

Oswald my gum!

Knock knock.
Who's there?
Thumping.
Thumping who?

Thumping creepy
is crawling up my leg!

Knock knock.
 Who's there?
Isabelle.
 Isabelle who?

Isabelle out of order?
 I had to knock.

Knock knock.
Who's there?
Boo.
Boo who?

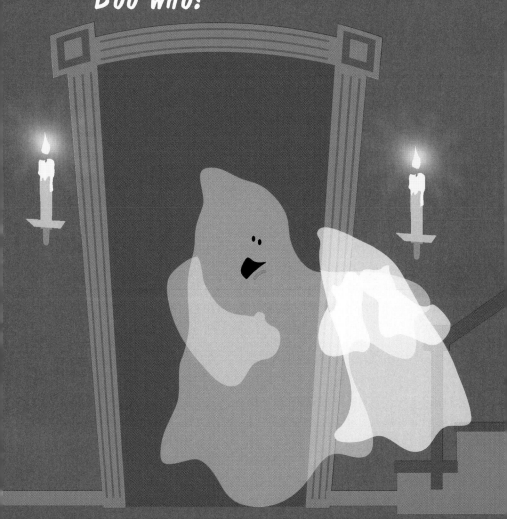

Why are you crying?

Knock knock.
    Who's there?
Police.
    Police who?

Police open up.
It's cold out here!

Knock knock.
  Who's there?
Elsie.
  Elsie who?

24   Elsie you later. Good-bye!